Ghosts of Talkeetna

Ghosts
of
Talkeetna

Sarah J. Birdsall
with
Jonathan Durr

A Northern Nights Book
Northern Nights Press
Talkeetna, Alaska

Published in Talkeetna, Alaska, by Northern Nights Press, P.O. Box 359, Talkeetna, Alaska, 99676.

Printed digitally in the United States of America.

Book design by Sarah J. Birdsall

ISBN 10: 0-615-84261-5
ISBN 13: 978-0-615-84261-5

For all who love Talkeetna, and for everyone who likes a good ghost story~

Contents:

Acknowledgments

Many, many thanks to all those without whose help this book would not have been possible: Jerry Stevens, Vicki Thompson, Joe Halladay, Bruce Hudson, Michele Faurot, Pam Allman, Trisha Costello, Mark Ashworth, Andrea Larson, Jake Graupman, Jean Armstrong, Gale Moses, Marty, Lynn and Evan Terstegge, Betsy Heilman, Roberta Sheldon, Deborah Vaughan, Cari Sayer, Dave Johnston, Kim Hoiby, Ken Marsh, Chris Mannix, Bill Barstow, Penny Johnson, Mary Farina, Sandy Shoulders, Johnny Baker, Shannon Nysewander, Tim Rose, Dean Cothran, Pat Pratt, Michael London, Charlie Loeb, Krista Maciolek, Whitney Wolff, and the Talkeetna Historical Society.

A big thank you to Jonathan Durr for helping write this book, to sister Beth for the song quote, and to Bill Barstow for *The Ghosts of Nantucket*. Additional thanks to Jennifer Birdsall for the photo opposite page 1 and for the photos on pages 60, 64, 88, 97, and 125, and to Bill Barstow for the photos on pages 12, 27, 28, 39, 66, 108, 114, 120, 132, 141 as well as on the front and back. All other photos by Sarah J. Birdsall.

Introduction

There are more things in heaven and earth, Horatio,
Than are dreampt of in your philosophy.

~William Shakespeare, *Hamlet*

For as long as I can remember, I have been fascinated by ghosts. In fact, one of the earliest—if not *the* earliest—memories I have involves a ghost, or at least what I have always thought was a ghost. I was three years old and my family had rented an old farmhouse in upstate New York that we called the "Bonnie Hill" house. My next to oldest brother, Jonathan, or "Boodey" as I called him, was a year and a half older than I was and we share this same memory: a little girl standing at the top of the stairs which led to the home's second floor attic. Whatever she was, whoever she was, we saw her together and remember the experience to this day. We saw her once, and never again.

But the fuzzy, watercolor memory still gives me goose bumps and makes the hairs on my arms stand on end. Literally. Whatever she was.

Throughout my growing years I enjoyed whatever good ghost stories I could find; years ago when my family moved to Alaska's remote Lake Iliamna, for instance, the children of our only neighbors, and hence our only playmates, told the following tale, which we called "The Ghost of Barney Green":

Barney Green was a disappointed miner who lived at Iliamna—in the same area as our neighbors—until his untimely death. One night our young friends—six in all—were home alone in their remote cabin and had the grand idea of sleeping in the root cellar. The cabin was built alongside a fast moving stream, which emptied into Iliamna, so the root cellar was cold and damp. However, kids being kids, they took their blankets and shut themselves into the musty quarters and eventually fell asleep. Sometime during the night the water table rose, flooding the cellar, and the children promptly left the space—except for one of the boys, Tommy, who slept soundly and was forgotten by the others. And he swore—during the time we knew him—that Barney Green had lifted him out of the root cellar and returned him to his safe dry bed. Barney Green who had been years in the grave.

Now, I could cross-examine him as an adult, but Tommy, along with his brother, Junior, met his own untimely death in the unforgiving waters of Lake Iliamna as a young man. An accident from which Barney Green did not appear and save him.

It was at Iliamna I had my second odd experience—and my first one as an adult. Like Tommy and Junior, their older sister, Dolores, had also died young—again in the unforgiving waters of Iliamna. Dolores and I had been particularly close—I looked up to her and admired her as if she were my own older sister; half Aleut and half white, she was beautiful with bright white teeth and thick dark brown braids and sparkling dark eyes; she was smart, and a champion sled dog racer who went to college then married a handsome pilot and returned to the country she loved. And she had been the first of the six children who would become our friends to greet us when my family arrived at Iliamna: as our boat, piloted by Dolores' father, an old friend of my own father, pulled up to Pope/Vannoy Landing where her family made their home, Dolores was there, smiling brightly and wearing tan jeans and hip boots, wading out to guide the boat to shore and eventually giving me a piggyback ride across the span of water to land. Years later she froze to death after falling into freezing water while trying to free her boat from forming ice. She was just 29 years old, and a young mother.

As her sister would later tell me, Dolores' two young daughters, who were left for days on the boat Dolores was trying to free as family, friends, and neighbors tried to reach the site, insisted they had not been alone. Their mother, they said, had been with them the entire time.

I was heartbroken at the news of Dolores' death, and several years afterwards I returned to Iliamna, a place I had not seen since the age of nine, as a journalist to interview Dolores' aging grandparents. As I stepped out of the mail plane onto the plane's floats where someone—who I don't remember—in hip-boots swung me to the shore, I looked down the beach and saw Dolores' grandmother, Patty, smiling and walking toward me, a young woman beside her. I could not believe my eyes. There was Dolores' face, her smile, her dark brown braids—coming down the beach. I stood there, speechless and shocked, my heart thundering in my chest. But as the women drew closer suddenly the face on the younger one shifted and it was no longer Dolores—it was a friend of Patty's, someone I didn't know.

Now we could analyze this—and analyze me—in many ways. But I always felt in my heart of hearts that Dolores had found a way to greet me on the shores of her beloved home one last time.

And there were times, yes, after my mother's death when I felt like she had come to me with words of comfort and words of advice, but it was a brief haunting in the summer of 2000, in my hometown of Talkeetna, by the spirit of a man I never knew in this world that convinced me beyond any doubt that there are ghosts among us. Of this, I am certain, and I don't even care about all the many—and quite good—arguments to the contrary. I was visited by a ghost, and this I know to be true.

So it has been with some satisfaction and of course with great attentiveness that I have noticed the recent popular interest in the subject in books like *The Ghosts of Nantucket* and *Nantucket Ghosts* by Blue Balliett, *Ghosts Among Us* by James Van Praagh, and *When Ghosts Speak* by Mary Ann Winkowski, for instance, as well as other books not only on the subject of "ghosts" but on the idea that death is not death, simply a transition, a belief mankind has fostered since the dawn of time. So why not ghosts?

But it's not for me—or anyone—to tell someone else how or what to believe or not to believe. And that's not the purpose of this collection: this collection is for fun. Because whatever else they may be, ghost stories are fun. It's as simple as that. And like New England towns such as Nantucket and Gloucester or southern towns such as Georgetown and Savannah, which have their ghost stories, my town of Talkeetna, Alaska, has its own. And here they are.

About Talkeetna:

Located in the Upper Susitna Valley, Talkeetna rests in a river-rich area surrounded by forests and shadowed by the massive Alaska Range, which on a clear day looks almost unreal in the not-so-distant distance, like a giant postcard plastered against the sky, McKinley, or Denali by its Native name, looming in its center. Summers in recent years have found Talkeetna bustling with visitors who walk the once quieter short span of Main Street visiting locally owned shops and restaurants, and the number of mountain climbers who pass through Talkeetna as they attempt the peaks of the Alaska Range in the spring and summer months has grown from roughly 680 in the late 1970s to 1,229 in 2012. Talkeetna also has a nationally recognized historic district, whose boundaries jag through the core of the main townsite, comprised of old buildings from the town's mining and trapping past.

The Talkeetna of my youth was far quieter than the Talkeetna of today; I remember numerous times, walking the twelve miles from my family's homestead "up the tracks" north of Talkeetna and entering, in the twilight of a late winter afternoon, a town that would be as still as if it, too, were as frozen as the ground, shrouded in white from the heavy snows, with a few windows faintly glowing as the lights within tried to beat back the descending dark. On these moments I would fight the urge to turn around and walk the long trail back home, where the little cabin by the lake would hold within its warm log walls my family, the friendly feel of the fire in the wood stove, and the comforting smell of whatever my mother was cooking for supper. While town seemed like a lonely land captured in a snow globe, home, by contrast, was like the picture on the syrup can. But in time Talkeetna would also become my home, and a still, quiet afternoon on Main Street is a long lost friend I am always happy to see.

Rumor (and there are plenty of rumors around here) has it that Talkeetna was an inspiration for the town of Cicely in the 1990s TV show, *Northern Exposure*. And well it may have been: we do have a radio station in the main townsite which was, until recently, housed in an old log cabin and to this day prides itself on its conglomeration of eclectic and mismatched local volunteer disc jockeys; also until recently we'd had, since the early '90s, a local doctor in the town (the business having changed hands once in the last twenty years); we have our historic Fairview Inn front and center on Main Street (though some might say the Latitude 62, located just on the edge of town, more resembles the Brick from the show); a trading post/grocery store which years ago also handled the local mail; a number of highly educated eccentric bush-rat characters not unlike the show's Adam (and I went to high school with an Ed or two); and yes, there is the occasional moose that wanders onto Main Street. And here as well stories abound: rivalries, love affairs, triumphs, failures, and escapades as we Talkeetna-ites live out our lives under the midnight sun on these streets and among these buildings that bear witness to our numerous goings-on or, as Samuel Taylor Coleridge put it so lovely in his poem, "Frost at Midnight":

This populous village! Sea, and hill, and wood,
With all the numberless goings-on of life,
Inaudible as dreams!

But instead of the sea, we have the rivers, and Talkeetna is, when all is said and done, a land of rivers. The Talkeetna River, which originates in the Talkeetna Mountain Range to the northwest, flows into the Susitna, which originates in the Alaska Range and whose waters were already joined by those of the Chulitna, a river whose origins lay somewhere between the two ranges. Together the rivers become the Big Susitna, or the Big Su, whose waters continue south toward Anchorage and the ocean waters of Cook Inlet.

The rivers were here when the Dghelay Teht'ana (Dena'ina) Indians, or the "Mountain People," fished their waters and dug cache pits to store their catch; the rivers were here when miners and trappers crossed their rushing waters on their way to Trapper Creek and the Petersville gold mines. The rivers were here when my family came in 1970 and settled on land north of town; the rivers will be here when we, like so many others, no longer will be.

And the rivers were here when the Alaska Railroad came to town in the early part of the 20th century, an entity which has been a large and looming presence in the community and its surrounding areas ever since. I can remember many cold frosty nights snuggled in my handmade wooden bed in my family's cabin and hearing night freights rumbling down the tracks two wooded miles away, heading north to Fairbanks or south to Anchorage, my imagination picturing their bright headlights cutting through the cold winter dark. Many were the mosquito filled rainy days in the summer or the toe-numbing winter hours I spent in my formative years along the railroad tracks waiting for the train. For us "up the tracks" residents, the train was postman, with packets of mail tossed from the partially open baggage car on the days it didn't stop, and on the days it did, the train brought along with the twice-weekly mail visitors or other woods-dwellers returning home from trips to town. The railroad established headquarters in Talkeetna for building the railroad in 1916, permanently altering the face of the town and its destiny and propelling the previously loosely organized settlement of miners, trappers, and Indians into a more structured community, with the ensuing tracks slicing through what could have been the middle of a larger main townsite but which instead divides into "east" and "west." Anyone who lives here is long used to the sound of the trains moving through, the whistle and the rumble, a recurring side note on the soundtrack of our lives.

Much has changed in Talkeetna since those times, from the "tent city" of the initial railroad days to the quiet unpaved Main Street of my youth to the busy little town it has become. A haunting—and one of my favorite—written descriptions of the town can be found in Nola Campbell's *Talkeetna Cronies*, a loving tribute to the legendary and at times notorious characters that roamed the area in days long since past and the buildings they inhabited. Campbell, who came to Talkeetna in 1939 and stayed for a little over a year, writes the following in her 1974 book:

"The deserted old log and frame buildings with their sagging roofs are slowly sinking into the ground. Windows are gone and doors are agape. They have stood the elements of time, the heavy rains and snow, the shifting of the ground and wearing away of the river's edge.

"The rivers race on as if trying to catch up with those who have gone on and to pay tribute to those hardy individuals who sacrificed modern life for pioneer hardships. They were a special breed.

"They mushed the trails, staked their claims, mined for gold, hunted the game, trapped the fur, caught the fish and proved up on the ground where they rest today. . ."

And as I think about those old buildings, and all of those who once lived within them that have passed on, I can't help but wonder who might still be here among us now.

The House Along
the Village Airstrip

The sound of footsteps on the stairs and across the second floor. Items falling off shelves for no reason. The feel of a sudden chill, and the reflection of a stranger in the window. . .anyone who's lived in Talkeetna for any length of time is familiar with the house along the village airstrip, and a good number of those may also have taken a turn living in the house at one time or another. And more still are very likely aware of the house's history—a very *haunted* sort of history that has woven its way into the folklore of the town.

A log structure built in various stages, the house sits quietly on a narrow road that parallels Talkeetna's historic village airstrip from which local pilots take off, land, and park the planes that, like the trains, are part of the fabric of daily Talkeetna life. Aging and rustic and hunkered into its spot like a solidly embedded stone, the house has changed hands and/or occupants numerous times over the past forty years. And with few exceptions, with each new owner, or each new tenant, the stories grew.

I lived in the house in the winter of 1976-77. I moved there in September from my remote home twelve road-less miles from town a week after school started in the local high school to board with a family friend so I, too, could go to school. Having been home-schooled since the third grade and now being a junior in high school, I was eager to see how "real" teenagers lived. So my family arranged for me to live with family friend Nita Kaufman and her two daughters, Sherri and Tekoa, who had recently moved into the house.

The house sat lengthwise along the street, and to enter the front door one had to approach the backside, facing the street, then swing around to where it went lengthwise along the inner yard. Old wooden steps led to a warped and rickety narrow porch, where a low door opened to the home's living area. The kitchen was in the prow of the house to the right, a bathroom was to the left, with the bottom of the stairs, also to the left, near the street side wall and leading upwards toward the center. My sleeping area was in a small landing at the top of the stairs, and here I would lay at night listening to the sounds of a house that were unfamiliar to a kid from the bush: the hum of the refrigerator in the kitchen, the rumble of the furnace down in the dark dank creepy basement. The sounds of plumbing. But the sound I noticed most of all during those long winter nights was the creak of footsteps on the old stairs, which always caused me to roll over on my cot to see who was approaching. And always there would be nothing, and no one, there.

I moved out mid-way through the winter and stayed with a friend who had a small trailer on her parents' property. Though before the end of the school year I returned to Nita's care, I still remember the strong feeling I had of wanting to be somewhere else for a while. This was partly due to the endless flux of people Nita had coming and going in the house; it always felt crowded to me. And it was also due to the fact that I was weary of being uncomfortable with my back to the stairs and feeling exposed and vulnerable in the area where I slept.

Penny Johnson moved into the house shortly after I left. "When I moved in, Sherri used to talk about how it had kind of bumps in the night and how you'd hear footsteps over the threshold into Nita's bedroom upstairs," Johnson says. One night when Nita was out, she and Sherri were sitting on the couch in the living room reading a story to Tekoa. "I don't know why, but I turned around and looked at the front door— which was maybe seven or eight feet away—and I said, 'He's here,' and at the same time I looked, the door flew open," she says. "It was a *feeling* before anything had actually happened—I didn't hear a sound, it was just a feeling. So we all went *oooo* and got silent because we wanted to hear the footsteps on the threshold over Nita's room. And it happened—we waited, I don't know, ten or twelve seconds, everyone holding their breath, and pretty soon we heard this *reee-eh, reee-eh, reee-eh*—some kind of footsteps went across her threshold. And that was, I mean I hate to say, the end of it—but we all sat there for a few minutes and didn't hear anything else—didn't hear any clumps or bumps and nothing ever happened again after I was there, but it was very real. . . it was very real to have me sense [the ghost] before it opened the door. My hair stood up before anything actually happened. I had the sensation that something was up."

Vicki Thompson, who lived in the house from 1984 to 1987, had what may be the most visually vivid experience. "I've actually seen a ghost, and that was an experience I believe I'll never forget," she says. "It was at night, and my cousin Sandy and I were sittin' in the living room. . .we were looking out through the window, and you could see the reflection of the living room in the window. We were sitting there talking; both of our dogs were sleeping by the stove—they were sound asleep—and we both were looking out the window and we saw this guy—he had dark hair, and he had on what I call a logging shirt—those blue and white checked kind of shirts—and Levi's and boots. We saw him in the reflection of the window, and we turned to look at the actual stairs and there was nothing there. And we turned back toward the window and it [the ghost] was going up the stairs. And both of our dogs at the same time instantly woke, and instantly ran toward the stairs, ridge hairs up and just growling and barking—I mean they were just spittin' spit everywhere and up the stairs they go. And it was all over quick, and they calmed right down. But she and I both knew we had seen something because the dogs did. But we could only catch its reflection in the window.

"And then it was like, do we stay, do we go—what do we do? But then, like I said, it all calmed down."

But even at that point Thompson was long used to odd things happening in the house. "The front door would always come open, *always* come open, whether it was locked or not," she says. "We'd get to the point that we'd say, 'If you're going to use the door, close it behind you,' which it/they never did.

"They woke me up in the middle of the night one night," Thompson remembers. "My bedroom window looked out over the Alaska Range—I could see Hunter, Foraker, and McKinley, right out my bedroom window. And so the first thing I'd do in the morning when I woke up was look out the window to see what kind of mood the mountain was in." One night she woke up unexpectedly and sat up in bed. "I know it was them—otherwise I don't know why I would have woken up in the middle of the night," she says. "But I looked out the window and the moon was hanging right over the eastern edge of McKinley and it was full, and it was huge, and it was orange and that whole mountain was just bathed in this beautiful orange glow—the whole mountain range. It was the most incredible sight I've ever seen in my life and I have yet to see anything like that since; it was intense. And they woke me up just so I could see that. I know it was them. There was no other reason for me to wake up."

Thompson says she always felt there was more than one ghostly resident in the house. "I do think there were several," she says. "And they'd play tricks; the lights would go out, come on, things would not be where you put them. . . I was doing dishes one time at the sink in the kitchen and for some reason I had my right hand down by my side for a minute and I felt my dog Socks licking my hand and I was pettin' his head and I looked down and there was absolutely nothing there—and I thought, holy shit." Thompson then went through the house to find the dog. "He was sound asleep in front of the stove.

"And Socks never liked going down into the basement," she continues. "He'd stand at the top of the stairs and growl and growl and scare the crap out of me. I thought, man, if you don't want to go down there, then I don't really want to go down there. But I had to sometimes because I'd have to light the hot water heater, but other than that, I'd try to stay out of the basement. It wasn't a bad place; it just gave me the willies. It was just weird. But the rest of the house was fun."

Fun? "It was a great house," she says. "I always thought the ghosts were nice, if that's possible—I never felt evil, or felt afraid. I felt protected, more or less, because I think they liked us. I've been sensitive to that kind of stuff all my life—I've just had weird things happen to me all my life. But that house—that house was great."

Longtime Talkeetna area resident Jerry Stevens, whose grandmother, Babe Barnes, owned the house in the early 1970s, says he believes the ghost—or one of the ghosts—may be that of Jacque "Farine" Batkin, who perished on McKinley during the first winter ascent of that mountain in 1967 and whose body was rumored to have been stored briefly in the home while waiting transport to Anchorage. However, the book about the historic climb, *Minus 148°*, written by climbing team member Art Davidson, states that Batkin's body was stored in the airplane hangar owned by legendary Talkeetna pilot Don Sheldon to hide it from the press while efforts were made to contact Batkin's family in France. But how long the body remained in the hangar, and if that was the only place it was stored, remains unknown.

The climber theory ties in nicely with reports from some residents of the house that the shades over the upstairs windows that face the Alaska Range would inexplicably snap open at first light; the local legend is that the ghost of a mountain climber (or, in some stories, multiple climbers) goes to these windows to see if the mountain was "out" and not shrouded in clouds—much the same as Thompson did when she lived there.

However, Stevens also reports that when his grandmother bought the property, the house was comprised solely of a small cabin to which Barnes attached a larger cabin that she had moved from another site; the second story was part of the new addition, added after Batkin's untimely death in what was to become a historic climb. In addition, lifelong Talkeetna resident Bruce Hudson says that when he was a kid, the larger cabin was on a site near where the Talkeetna Post Office now is, and that there were "definitely ghosts in there. I don't know who they were," he says. "That was when I was pretty young."

But regardless of the ghost's (or ghosts') identity, far too many stories have emerged from the house to be ignored. Stevens relates the following story of his late grandmother's:

"While Grandmother was fixing the place up, she had a plumber run lines for the water. He went outside to get something and went back down to the basement and a few minutes later he came running out of the basement, packed his stuff up and left. Well, Babe called him back a few days later and asked why he was not going to finish the job. He told her that [after leaving the basement to get some solder] when he went back down to put a section of pipe together, he found that somebody had already put the pipe together, and he swore that he did not do it. He flat-out told her, 'You, little lady, have a ghost and I do not want to go down there again.' So she hired somebody else to finish the job.

"She also had a cat that loved to go down there and every now and then she would hear the cat growl and carry on. And she had a dog that refused to go down there at all."

Andrea Larson, who bought the house in 1995, had heard the stories but moved into her new home a non-believer. Until a flying pancake gave her second thoughts.

"People would talk about a cold chill then hearing footsteps walking across the upstairs," Larson says. "And then Babe used to hear shades flip up in the upstairs bedroom. The shades would flip up for no reason." And while she found the stories unusual—and had also noticed the door would occasionally pop open on its own after being securely shut—things didn't really connect for her, she says, until after the pancake incident.

"I was making pancakes—making breakfast—and my husband Alan walked in behind me and started talking to me. I was half consciously getting ready to flip over the pancake and suddenly whoop! it flipped up over my shoulder. I turned around, picked up the pancake off the floor and threw it back in the pan and started talking again and Alan said, 'What? How did you do that?' And I said, 'I didn't do anything.' And he said, 'That was weird' and pointed out how the pancake just sort of went flying.

"And that's what happened. It was very odd, but we didn't have cold chills or anything, it was more like, *that was very odd.*"

Larson's eldest son, Jake Graupman, has his own memories of his years in the house. "It was fun; my friends and I always went on hunts for ghosts—we were always in the basement trying to find something," he says. "It was a cool basement—there were always creaks in there and shadows—it was a really scary house." Noting that he found being in the downstairs living area alone particularly creepy ("It was always creaking; there was always something like a cabinet door opening. . ."), Graupman describes a time when he and his friend, David Nelson, saw something they couldn't quite explain:

"One time we were sitting there and a cabinet door opened and a glass flew out—there was a shelf beneath the cabinet and the glass missed the shelf completely and shattered all over the floor," he says. "It had to move out from the cabinet to miss the shelf. . .it was weird." There had been no external factors—an earthquake, or an exceptionally large vehicle on the road outside—to explain the glass' sudden leap from the shelf.

"Every time I talk to someone [about the house] they say something," Larson says. "When you put all those stories together, it is unusual—all these incidents."

In 1999, Larson sold the house to her mother,

Jean Armstrong (who contends her daughter made no mention of any extra inhabitants at the time of the sale). Armstrong quickly renovated the old building and opened a bed and breakfast, Talkeetna Landings B&B.

Much to Armstrong's disappointment, the door no longer opened on its own, the shades didn't whip upwards at sunrise, and there were no flying pancakes or mysterious footsteps on the stairs and on the second floor. But she does have this: one night she was downstairs watching TV and heard a loud thump! coming from upstairs. Upon investigation, she found a mess. "The dresser was thrown to the floor and there were clothes all over the place," she says. A friend would later tell her it was a parting gift from the ghosts, as she was set to leave the house the next day.

Carrying on the family tradition, another of Armstrong's daughters, Gale Moses, and her journalist husband, John, bought the house from her in 2006. Like Armstrong, they found the house much quieter than it had been in its reputed rambunctious past. "I heard many different stories about the house, but I never really experienced anything," says Moses.

Armstrong wonders if perhaps her renovations were disliked by the house's ghostly inhabitant(s) and inspired him or them to move on. "I might have missed a whole lifetime of ghost memories," she laughs. With the house having recently undergone yet another sale, time will tell if its mysterious inhabitant—or inhabitants—has, as you might say, given up the ghost.

The Three German Bachelors' Cabin

Alone at night in my Talkeetna home writing up ghost stories is a sometimes unsettling thing to do: the house seems way too quiet, despite the happy warm sound of the wood burning stove, and the dark outside the windows seems infinite and immeasurable, like an endless ocean of dark blue air. I jump a little at every unexpected sound. And it seems, thus far in my exploration of Talkeetna's haunted history, it's the stories from the Three German Bachelors' Cabin that unsettle me the most. A small and dark log building located just at the beginning of Talkeetna's Main Street, the cabin was built in the 1930s for a man named Frank Moennikes, who owned the Fairview for a time and who shared the cabin with two brothers, Tony and Henry Meise. Together the three bachelors inspired the name by which the building is still known today.

Now owned and maintained by the Talkeetna Historical Society, in the years between this and its German brothers origins the cabin provided shelter for numerous area residents. One of these was a man nicknamed "Eight Ball" who died unexpectedly and somewhat mysteriously in the cabin in the late 1960s and was found in his cot one morning by his friend, Rhevis Cothran; another was my brother, Jonathan Durr, who lived there with friends as a teen in the 1970s and who is among those residents rendered more than a bit uncomfortable by the uneasiness within the cabin's walls. Jonathan writes the following:

~~*~~

Alaska is a scary place. It's immense, remote, harsh, unforgiving, and mysterious. Every village has its stories: disappearances, murders, unexplained deaths and all the tragedies one could imagine from a harsh frontier.

Alaska Natives have a malevolent spirit for every season. There's the Windigo, Uuiliriq, and dozens of others. These spirits, demons, and monsters lay in wait to ambush unwary travelers or lost hunters, and thus explain the many disappearances that occur in the lonely expanses of the far north.

Every village has its shadowy stories and secrets. Every village also has a cabin with a dark history, a place that just doesn't feel right. A place to which adults give a wide berth on moody dark nights.

In Talkeetna, the story was the mysterious death of a long ago resident nick-named "Eight Ball;" the place was the Three German Bachelors' Cabin, and it was where he died. The cabin sits low and dark in the heart of "Beautiful Downtown Talkeetna," within sight of the historic Fairview Inn, which was Eight Ball's favorite haunt (no pun intended).

Eight Ball was found dead in the Three German Bachelors' Cabin after a night of debauchery at the Fairview. Eight Ball was a young man and the cause of his death was never verified—at least to anyone's satisfaction. So the rumors started: enemies, adulterous affairs, mob connections from his past, etc. What also began were strange happenings in the cabin where he died. So much, in fact, that by the time I moved to the area as a boy, it was common local lore that the dark cabin was haunted. I remember looking at it one stormy night and feeling a chill run up my spine. I made a mental note to avoid that cabin whenever possible. Little did I know that I was one day to be a part of the Eight Ball ghost saga.

Since my family lived remote—out of town and off the road system—in order for me to go to high school, I had to board with friends in town. During my sophomore year I boarded with my friend, Mark. This was a great situation except that Mark lived in the Three German Bachelors' Cabin which, as I said, gave me the creeps.

I was excited about living in town, though, and going to school. However, from the beginning I didn't feel good in the cabin. I always spent Friday nights at my friend Pete's house, and as the weeks went by I started counting the days until Friday as I was becoming more and more uncomfortable in the cabin. And things had started happening.

The first strange thing that occurred involved the radio. One night I woke up and the radio was on, which puzzled me as I felt sure I had turned it off before going to bed. Several nights later it happened again. As the weeks passed this began happening more and more frequently.

One night I woke up and my attention was drawn to a cot on the far side of the cabin. This was where our friend Skip slept when he was around. I saw a figure sitting on the cot and assumed it was Skip. "Hey, Skip," I said, then rolled over to go back to sleep. There was no reply, but I didn't think much of it.

The next morning, however, I noticed that the cot had not been slept in. I asked Mark what had happened to Skip. Mark informed me that Skip was still in Anchorage and would not be back for another day. So who was the mysterious figure sitting silently on the cot?

The last straw for me came shortly after the afore-mentioned incident. Along with the radio, the single bare light had begun to turn on and off by itself. It was a ceiling fixture operated with a pull cord. I was sitting alone one night reading and the light went out. I turned it back on and it went out again. I turned it back on and a few minutes later it turned off again. Only this time I could actually hear the cord being pulled. I ran out of the cabin in absolute terror.

Unfortunately, the story does not end on that dark night. Mark continued to live in the cabin for another five or six years. He never talked about what happened, but at some point he had an experience in the cabin that scared him to death.

He left Talkeetna for good shortly after. He simply told his friends that something had happened in the cabin and that he couldn't stay. He never came back and I never saw him again.

I have since suspected that a malevolent force, a discarnate entity, may have attached itself to Mark and went with him and tormented him. I heard that his life was not going good—drinking and depression. A mutual friend talked to him and he simply stated that because of Eight Ball he could never return to Talkeetna. The last word I heard about Mark was that he had fallen out of contact with everyone, including family, and was feared dead.

Every time I walk by that low dark cabin on the corner I shudder. Then I ask the question I've asked over and over during the past thirty years: "Mark, what happened? What did you see? What did the specter tell you?" Sadly, I fear Mark took these dark secrets to the grave.

~~*~~

In January 2012, roughly a year after this story was written, we learned that Mark perished that month in a cabin fire somewhere in rural Nevada—alone and still estranged from family and friends.

Joe Halladay is another longtime area resident who wouldn't argue the idea that there was, at least at one time, a presence in the Three German Bachelors' Cabin. And, like others before him, he found it to be a presence most unfriendly.

Halladay came to Talkeetna in the mid 1970s, and sometime not long after found himself staying occasionally at the Three German Bachelors' Cabin. "I just had a backpack thrown upstairs and was floppin' down on whatever was up there," he says. During this time he was seeing a young local woman, Shelly, and once when she was there her stepfather showed up at the door with an ax, yelling for his stepdaughter. Though Shelly complied and the confrontation ended without incident, and though he can't remember for certain if his experience with the cabin's presence occurred that very night, Halladay links the two events together and wonders if the unease created by his girlfriend's angry parent helped set the scene for what followed when he slept in the cabin's loft.

"I just absolutely flashed awake," he says. "When I lay down, I go to sleep—probably within two minutes of when I lay down to go to bed. I don't stay up and linger or anything. And I sleep nine, ten hours easily. . .And I just flashed awake. And I could absolutely feel that there was a presence, right there. It was like—you're wanting to almost hide from somebody and be quiet, and be hidden, because you were scared, and I just laid there and I was like—scared. And there was no sound or any kind of disturbance of any kind, just this overwhelming presence. This feeling of a presence, right next to me. And I just laid there, motionless. And it might have went on for—I don't know; I can't really remember because it's been so long—a minute or maybe a little more—and then it was gone.

"And I think a lot of times the doors slamming, and noises and things that are related to things supernatural or they think are spirit oriented, are like these triggers, like some sort of signal, but I don't think that's really very accurate," Halladay continues. "It's more a feeling of presence." In the years since, Halladay has spent time contemplating ideas of what's "real."

"You want to count on things that you can count on—like what is, *is*, but what about what isn't?" he says. "We don't connect much with what isn't, but what *isn't* is as important as what is. . .And I think in spiritual things, that sometimes it's very obscure. And it knocks, and you're trying to figure it out, is it real, is it not, is it like a hint, is it a signal, is it a—what is it? And it's almost like there's this sort of big floating wall that insulates against those kinds of things, and sometimes they come through it. And you're like, what was that? Because it's very difficult to identify." But there was nothing subtle, he says, in what he felt on that long ago night in the cabin. "In my instance, I was terrified."

Halladay also shared a recent experience he'd had at a radar station on the North Slope where he works. Years ago a fellow "sloper" had told him about hearing voices while in the middle of nowhere—a low murmur of men's voices, "more of a tone rather than deciphering what they were saying."

One day Halladay was out snowshoeing, and suddenly he heard what had been described to him years ago. "I heard this low-pitched sound of men talking," he says. "And then it was gone."

Ghosts of Talkeetna~39

Clarence

It was the early morning of what was to be a hot summer day, the kind where the sky is a bright shade of light blue and the air is filled with the smell of warm green leaves and the sound of insects in the brush. Kim Hoiby, asleep in her small dwelling on a wooded lot along a quiet road, remembers waking when she heard the shot ring out but figured it was a neighbor, target practicing or chasing a bear out of a yard. But instead it was her elderly friend, Clarence Miller, taking his own life a short distance up the road. Clarence had been diagnosed with terminal lung cancer, and his days as a woodsman at his cabin north of Talkeetna, a life that he treasured, were over.

Hoiby, who got to know Clarence when, as the wife of his neighbor, she, too, lived in the bush north of town, was doing all she could to care for her old friend in the face of his illness and recalls how, the night before he died, he was un-talkative and withdrawn. "I'd just gotten him out of the hospital about two weeks before—he was going down fast—and Clarence wouldn't hardly speak to me that night," she says. "He'd been planning this, I'd decided."

That morning, when she realized Clarence wasn't on the property and her walking stick was also gone, she ran down the road and found him, not thinking at first that he was dead. "I thought he'd passed out," she says, but then she "put two and two together," the early morning gunshot a haunting, foreboding echo she wouldn't soon forget.

Devastated, Hoiby left town for a while, heading to a small town farther north along the George Parks Highway where she had also lived for a number of years. "I was pretty much in shock, and I went to Cantwell," she says. "But I had to come back; I had a lot of stuff to do there." Not wanting to be there alone, she had her friend Bev go over to the property with her. "This was a couple of weeks after it had happened," she says. "This was the first incident. I was climbing up the stairs [to the loft]; well, half my body was above the floor and the other half was down below. And I kept feeling this on my pant leg"—here she pulls on the bottom of her faded blue jeans—"and I said, 'What, Bev?' And she yelled at me from outside and she said, 'Did you call me?' Okay, and I'm like, *What the hell?* Anyway, this had happened like three times. And it was definitely a tug-tug on the bottom of my pants. That was way weird, and being there creeped me out anyway; it took me a year to be able to stay in that house again.

"So instead I started staying in my travel trailer that was up there. And it was probably the same week; I wasn't sleeping well and it was summer, a lot of daylight, and I was reading in my bed in the trailer. And I heard a bump, then didn't hear anything, and I was laying back reading and the blankets were up here"—over her chest—"bunched up, and I could see and feel the blanket press down that much, just touching me. It happened again—it went down and up—there was no hand there. But that's what it was doing. And my heart started beating really fast and I was thinking, *This isn't happening, I'm dreaming,* and I grabbed myself and inflicted pain, to where I bruised myself, and it happened a third time. There was something touching me and pushing on me. . .I knew it was Clarence.

"I never had another incident after that, just those two. They were actually physical—it wasn't the cold breeze that would blow through; you can make excuses for that, but I can't make any excuses for the physical pulling and tugging on my pants and then the actual seeing and feeling—seeing with my own eyes—the blankets go down, like somebody's doing that to you. And then I knew that it was Clarence, and I wasn't even scared once it dawned on me what was happening."

Hoiby says the two incidents inspired her to do some reading about the spiritual nature of ghost encounters, and she talked to a friend who told her about the Tibetan belief that the soul lingers for a variable time after death before moving on. "That gave me some thought," she says. "So okay—don't close your mind off."

Jonathan wrote a tribute to Clarence after his death where he described Clarence's decades-ago decision to leave New York City and his occupation as a plumber and head for the wilderness, where he found a new life for himself. The tribute (originally published in the *Talkeetna Times*) reads, in part, as follows:

Clarence Miller lived the first forty odd years of his life in New York City. He dreamed of Alaska since childhood, but being the youngest son in his family he was obligated to care for his mother until she died. Clarence worked as a plumber for some twenty years. During this time, he studied and planned for the life he would lead as an Alaskan backwoodsman. He read everything he could get his hands on regarding outdoor skills, cabin building, putting up food, etc.

His 20s and 30s passed as he lived the life of a New York City plumber but continued to dream of a life far away. It must have been hard for him during those decades. Upon his mother's death, he was free to begin the adventure of his life. He loaded his Pontiac with the things he would need in his new life, pointed it north and left New York City behind. He never went back.

This is when our trails crossed. Clarence was able to obtain five remote acres from the State of Alaska three miles from where my family lived. After a decade of living in the Alaskan bush, my family had seen our share of "pilgrims" or, as we call them in Alaska, "Cheechakos," come and go. Many of them came to the bush with big plans, full of enthusiasm. However, the reality of minus 50° degree weather, bears and mosquitoes, put an end to their wilderness adventures. For many, the hard work of bush life is too much.

Clarence, however, had been dreaming of living the life of an Alaskan bush dweller for decades. He was well prepared. He had all the tools he would need and most of all he had the knowledge. He built a lean-to, set up a nice camp and began building his cabin. He used all hand tools for building and was a gifted craftsman. In fact, Clarence never did acquire a chainsaw.

In short order Clarence became one of the most skilled, resourceful backwoodsman I'd ever known. He lived primarily off the land. He grew a wonderful vegetable garden, harvested all the wild plants and berries available in our area, and fished and hunted for his meat. He knew how to preserve his foodstuffs through canning and smoking. Plus, he had a huge root cellar in which he was able to store his garden vegetables—such as potatoes, beets and turnips to name a few—through the long winter. In short, he lived like a king.

~~*~~

And perhaps, in those woods he used to roam, he still does.

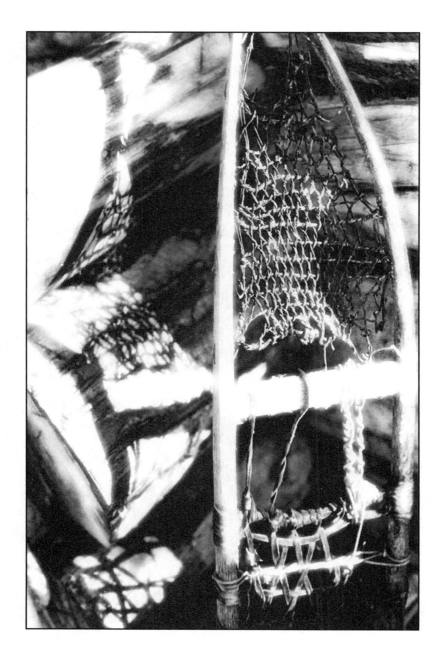

Once in a Blue Moon

"It was on the very first night we were there," says Marty Terstegge. His wife, Lynn, nods her head and adds: "It was on a blue moon—you know a blue moon on New Year's Eve is every nineteen years, so it was the New Year's blue moon which would have been twenty-one years ago from now. It was December 31^{rst}, 1990."

This night was the beginning of the Terstegge's Talkeetna adventure. They had come to town from Anchorage to spend the night in the Talkeetna Roadhouse, which was closed that winter and up for sale, the previous owners having moved on to other things. Lynn and Marty had spent a different night there two years previous and had, at that time, ruminated of someday owning a place like that themselves. By an odd combination of serendipitous events, they had run into the current owner and were granted the invitation to go "root around the place" as Marty says, to see if they might really like to own it. So, with their two small children, Katie and Evan, in tow, they stepped down through a tunnel of that winter's deep snow to get to the door on that New Year's Eve and entered their future home. And as incredible as their story of that night is, it may be even more incredible that within a week they would make an offer on the place—ghosts and all.

It began with an old 1940s Rockola Jukebox that caught their eye as they settled themselves in for the night. "We were done, we were all in our pajamas, just kind of milling around down in the living room," Marty says. He decided to see if the Rockola still worked. "I pulled it out, plugged it in and low and behold, it lit up and so I dropped a nickel in it and we picked a song."

"I think it was 'Blue Danube,'" says Lynn.

Marty nods. "'Blue Danube' the waltz came on and Katie and Evan, in their pj's, were weaving around to the music and Lynn and I were standing next to the jukebox looking at them, and we just both kind of froze, and both looked at one another at the same time and I said, 'Did you just see what I saw?' She said, 'Yeah.'

"It was wisps of smoke," Marty continues. "That's the only way I can describe it. It just kind of puffed and swirled up through the floor and coalesced into couples which were dancing around the room, around the kids."

"There were three couples," Lynn says. "The smoke swirled up out of the floor, and all of a sudden, through the swirls, you could see that there were six people, three couples, just dancing. And they started going around and probably made not even half a circle around the room. . .they were dancing with themselves and the whole group was going around and then it just kind of went—just went away."

"The kids never noticed it," Marty says. "They just kept dancing around in the middle of it."

"I wouldn't have believed it, if he hadn't seen the exact same thing," Lynn says. "You're just astonished, dumbfounded, after seeing something like that."

Despite that unusual first night, the Terstegges wasted no time buying the Roadhouse and making it their home. And life was fairly normal, though the building had, as Marty says, "a lot of noises—doors and windows sounding like they were screeching open, doors opening and banging" and there were some places that didn't feel quite right.

"The hallway was the worst—the long hallway going down to the bathrooms and the laundry room," son Evan adds. "Every single time my sister and I went down to go to the bathroom we'd run as fast as we could. We just had a bad feeling, and it'd be dark behind us; there was a big heating duct and a lot of noises coming from that. Our hair would stand up on end, we'd get the shivers and have to take off running."

"The only place I ever felt creepy was down that long hallway," Lynn agrees.

But there were still two hard-to-explain events yet to come. For Lynn, a second ghostly incident occurred one day when no one else was around. Marty had recently removed boards off of the walls going up the stairs so the original logs were exposed, and one day Lynn was standing at the top of the stairs admiring the historic handiwork. "I was looking at those logs, and at the burlap that was twisted between them for chinking," she says. "It was just so kind of romantic in the sense that they used what they had; it was fascinating that they'd do something like that." But as she looked, what she was seeing started to shift. "All of a sudden, in that same wispy kind of foggy smoky way, I saw these hands, these old hands, twisting that burlap. I focused in on it, and I saw maybe two or three twists of the hands and then it was gone again. I would have really doubted myself on that, too, if it hadn't been visually similar to what Marty and I had seen with the fog—I remember it vividly."

"And I've had them talk to me down in the crawl

space under there," Marty says. He says that one time he and a friend, Wes, went down under the building to fix something. "I sent him [Wes] back up top to go get a tool—I think I was working on some plumbing and I heard him, I thought, right beside me saying, 'Move over.' And I'm like, 'What are you going to do?' And [a voice said], 'Just move over.' So then I turned around and looked, and Wes wasn't there. He'd gotten lost, as a matter of fact: he'd gone back and he'd crawled under the trap door that was open and went past it toward Main Street. And he'd turned and went under the kitchen to where you just couldn't go any farther." Marty then heard his friend calling for him and crawled toward him with a light so Wes could get out, temporarily forgetting the strange presence that had been beside him in Wes' absence.

"'Move over'—I don't know what was going on with that," Marty says with a laugh. "Somebody crawling under there telling me to move over."

The Terstegges owned, operated, and lived in the Roadhouse, which has been central to Talkeetna daily life since the already existing building was turned into a roadhouse in 1944, until they sold it in 1996 with no further encounters with dancing ghosts or working hands or voices in the dark.

"I don't remember anything specifically strange

other than those events," Lynn says. "Nothing ever fell off the walls or jumped off the shelves or anything like that. And that was all toward the very beginning when we first lived there. Other than going down the hallway—I rarely went down there; I just really didn't like the hallway in the dark. When you say you're scared of the dark, you know—what's in the dark that makes you scared?"

"It's not *knowing* what's in the dark," Marty says.

"You just never know," Lynn adds.

Indeed. And the Terstegges can testify to that.

Current Roadhouse owner Trisha Costello, who has "lived and worked" at her establishment at "all hours of the day and night" states that she can honestly say that she's never had a ghost encounter. But "Wait. . ." she adds. "One thing comes to mind. I have a print of [Talkeetna artist] Jim Gleason's triple panel, 'Ascension of Ray Genet,' and one day it hurled itself off the wall and broke the glass." Genet was a world renowned mountain climbing guide who lived in and worked out of Talkeetna for many years until his death on Mt. Everest in 1979. "In fact," Costello continues, "I still need to get the glass replaced. At the time it seemed a little odd and spooky. . .but it ended there."

But perhaps the next time a blue moon falls on a cold dark New Year's Eve and someone plays an old song, there will be another story to tell~

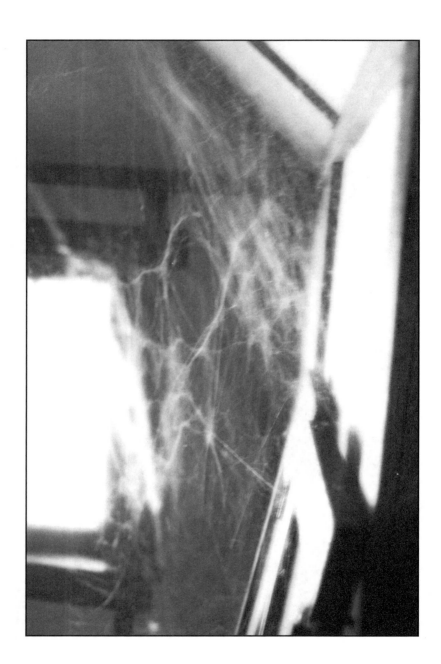

The Beautiful Green House on Main Street

The Weatherell house has sat alongside Talk-eetna's Main Street since 1940, when it was built by a Norwegian log smith named Elmer Ronning for a man named Tom Weatherell. As a child and later as an adult, I always found the painted green logs and the cottagey look of the place enchanting, even though the old home had long been deserted; these thoughts were confirmed when once I interviewed a woman named Eleanor Trepte Seitze Martin, who grew up in Talkeetna in the 1930s and '40s and who told me that after it was built, the Weatherell house was her favorite place to visit.

And maybe the house is now a favorite of other types of visitors.

"It was probably early evening or something like that," says Talkeetna resident Shannon Nysewander. "I was going by the Weatherell house, taking dogs down to the river, and I looked up in the top window and there was a shadow and it was like somebody was up there. I just kind of stopped and I looked and it

moved again and I thought, 'Oh, that's weird, I wonder who's there?' There weren't any cars around, and it looked like it had been closed up for awhile, and so I just kept walking."

When renovations on the building began in the summer of 2011, dust and an elegant collection of cobwebs were evidentiary to the idea that no one had, indeed, been in the upstairs for quite some time. But that wouldn't surprise Nysewander, who says she's seen ghosts before on a haunted property in San Diego, California, and says she takes such things for granted. "My mom was from England," she says. "Her family lived in an old house and every morning they'd come down and everything in the house was rearranged—they had a poltergeist. For our family it's pretty much normal."

And Talkeetna, she says, "is what it is—an old town. A lot of old buildings."

In the Darkness With Ray

My very favorite memory of the famed mountain climber Ray Genet, who first conquered Mt. McKinley in the 1960s and in the years between that time and the time of his death on Mt. Everest in 1979 became a facet of Talkeetna life, occurred on a July day sometime in the mid 1970s. It was "Moose Drop" weekend, formerly known as the Talkeetna Moose Dropping Festival, an event that occurred faithfully on the second weekend in July from the early '70s until 2009, when it became clear the festival had outgrown our limited townsite and it was decided to give the festival a rest. This particular festival was back when event participants were the people that lived in or near Talkeetna, with activities (highlighted by the famed Moose Drop Toss game) largely occurring in the span of one day. This memory comes from the end of one such day, the end of another Moose Drop, with a dusty Main Street thinning out and quieting as friends and neighbors wandered home while temperamental-looking clouds invaded the partly sunny sky. I found myself walking on the edge of the Village Park, across the street from the B&K (now Nagley's), noticing—and delighting in—the sudden stormy feel to the wind. I stopped to watch the trees sway and the dust swirl in the semi-deserted center of town and noticed I was not alone: standing a short distance from me, over near the Three German Bachelors' Cabin, was Ray Genet, hands on his hips and smiling away. Then the wind picked up the dust on the street and spun it around, forming a mini-tornado that whipped past us both. As I watched the twirling dust ball collapse and fizzle, I felt eyes on me and looked over at Ray. "You like the stormy weather, eh?" he said, and we shared a smile at having witnessed that small demonstration of nature's fury before gong our separate ways to find shelter from the imminent rain.

And years later, when Ray Genet failed to return from his Everest climb, I think we all knew we had lost something similar to that perfect little fury that spun down the street that July day—something fascinating and wild, and all too quickly gone.

Does part of Ray Genet still linger in the places he haunted while alive? Betsy Heilman thinks yes, maybe something does—

"I remember *very* clearly the whole event," says Heilman, a local artist. After living in Talkeetna for a number of years and miraculously surviving cancer and suffering the loss of her longtime sweetheart, Heilman found herself working at a local lodge located along the shores of the Susitna River. A former climbing partner of Genet's owns the lodge. "I never knew him," Heilman writes, referring to Genet, "but from what I hear he was larger than life in every way, from a handshake like steel—a grasp that one would never forget if given the chance to shake his hand—to a mind like a trap, as my mother would say, one that never forgot a thing and was never distracted by entertainment or glamour. I do, however, know his son Taras well, and to this day, my lively friend is as fierce, tenacious, and warm as a person can possibly be. From what I hear, Ray's intuition was sharp and forever un-derailed by our culture's every effort to squish personal insight and power."

And it was Ray Genet who came to Heilman's mind as she worked at the lodge and, at times, felt as if she was not alone. She writes the following:

"From the very beginning I had this weird feeling whenever I was at the lodge. You know, like a tingling in the spine that widens the eyes and makes you feel hypersensitive.

"The lodge is very well kept, on the shore of the Big Su. The riverfront location has big windows and fishing right out the door. The location is perfectly set for a Talkeetna adventure and now serves hundreds of tourists every summer. Frank [Genet's friend and climbing partner] and Ray bought the riverfront parcel in the early '70s. At the time, to get to Talkeetna, one either went by rail or drove an unpaved road fourteen miles from the George Parks Highway.

"Originally, the two camped in tents on the river's edge and eventually each built a house, from scratch and by hand, on the property. The lodge became Frank's after Ray's death on Everest. There are photos and relics in Ray's honor on the walls and shelves in the office, living room, and throughout the lodge.

"In my first weeks of work, on several occasions, I could hear someone coming in the front door. I would go downstairs to see who was there and the door would be open, but no one was there. When I was downstairs I would hear someone walking upstairs, and go up to see, or call out, finding still that I was alone. There is a closet with wooden panels in the upstairs hallway where a person could sleep on the floor. The space is not as tall as a person, but just wide enough for a bedroll and mostly empty but for a few old sheets and a vacuum. Rarely did anyone stay there. Often I would find the doors to the small nook open.

"I continued about my business regarding any incident as a normal thing for an Alaskan lodge, suffering minus 40° and ice jams, 15- 20 feet of snow and lots of different kinds of travelers passing through. Until one day. . .

"There is an attached garage where the second set of laundry machines are. . . on this particular day I heard the sound of the front door opening several times and found the door open more than once. No one was there. No sign of a human being, no dirt on the floor, nothing but the door open a crack and a cold breeze wafting into the kitchen/living room area. At one point I walked into the garage to get a 33-gallon trash bag. I had both the washer and dryer churning away. The lights were all on and a small digital clock was on top of the washer showing the time in red light. I don't remember exactly what time it was, but let's say 2:30. I reached for the box of trash bags on the housekeeping supplies bottom shelf, pulled the black plastic from the box and stood and turned toward the center of the garage to open the bag so I could put it in the can and fill it with trash. If one has any experience with a 33 gallon trash bag just out of the box, they know that you must pull it apart a little, put a corner into each hand and quickly and sharply flap the bag in the air so that the sides come apart; the bag fills with air and can be placed into the trash can. In the instant that I flapped the bag the garage went dark. The lights went off, the washer and dryer stopped, there was no buzz from the freezer and the clock went black. The room was dead silent. My heart slammed against my chest, skipped a beat, and my hairs stood on end. In a millisecond of terror I flapped the bag again and the garage was back to life.

"Having had a few encounters with the supernatural in the past, I gathered myself quickly. In the next second or two I thought to myself, 'OK, that might have been a coincidence, maybe the static electricity from the bag caused some kind of electro-magnetic reaction in the garage. This is a good opportunity to practice what little I know of ghost encounters.' My fear passed and my curiosity set in. With my awareness at its peak, I stood very still and spoke out loud saying, 'Ray, if that's you, do it again, or tell me what you want.' I raised my arms and flapped the bag again, and again the room went dark and silent. I was stunned almost silly and looked around eagerly in the stillness and dark, listening to hear a voice or see someone at the door. I paused and said out loud again, 'Tell me what you want'; no response. Deliberately and without scrutiny I waved the bag into the air again and the lights went back on, the washer and dryer both continued without me having to press any buttons, and the clock read 2:30, no flashing red 12:00, just as if it had never turned off. I hesitated a second or two, thought that no one would ever believe me, and simply stepped over to the garbage can to put the 33-gallon bag in its proper place.

"This was one of the most direct events I ever had with a ghost. I feel a tingle in my spine and a rise in my stomach as I write the story. Although he never spoke to me, somehow through the windows of time I feel that just once Ray and I have met, and I am honored."

And the Party Goes On: The Historic Fairview Inn

I have often wondered this: If the walls of the Fairview could talk, what stories would they tell?

The historic Fairview Inn has sat prominently in the center of town, like a beating heart, since the 1920s when it was built by a man named Ben Nauman, the first in a long line of owners. Throughout the years it has been home-away-from-home for many—too many, perhaps, as the lure of its lighted windows on a cold and quiet winter night has long offered the promise of companionship and camaraderie in this northern town. I myself have many memories from within those walls: late fall 1973, when my family's cabin up the tracks burned down, leaving us with nothing but the clothes we were wearing and a beat-up old station wagon we'd had parked in town, and we held a fund-raiser there at which my father and my brothers played guitars and sang all night while the townspeople proved more generous than we could have ever imagined; Talkeetna's longtime softball team, the Mandingos, in their red team shirts doing their infamous beer slide across the old wooden floors after a victorious local tournament; my long divorced parents, the year before my mother died, dancing across the floor, their synchronized movements a testament to the many years they had spent together; birthdays, weddings, memorials, numerous conversations with friends and neighbors as time moves forward and the Fairview remains, as constant as the rivers.

So. If those walls could speak, there would be tales of joys and sorrows, friendships and rivalries, fights (the Fairview has seen a few of those), summit-of-the-mountain celebrations, late nights where local bands rocked the walls and dancers shook the floors, quiet afternoons with one or two patrons hunched over drinks at the bar.

And maybe there would be other tales—tales of patrons who never left. "The Fairview is so haunted," says Shannon Nysewander, who worked at the Fairview a number of years ago and says she would catch glimpses of old patrons who had passed away. "You're working late and you catch somebody sitting there at the bar out of the corner of your eye. . .you're working in the back room and you hear somebody out there and then you'll go check and nobody would be there, or you would catch a glimpse then kind of look, and they're not there," she says.

"That was my experience, too," says Mary Farina, who worked at the Fairview in the 1980s. "I'd be closing up and out of the corner of my eye I'd see somebody then I'd go to look and there'd be nobody there—but what I'd seen was a solid person, a solid figure." There was one ghost in particular that she would see and was told it was the ghost of a man nicknamed Eight Ball (who is also suspected of haunting the Three German Bachelors' Cabin); however, not knowing what Eight Ball (whose real name was said to be Charles Gallope, and who I've not been able to find any substantial information on) looked like, it could have been any of the bar's past residents whose spectral forms have reportedly been seen in their old haunt.

"The ghost of Jim Shaff's been there for a long time," says lifelong Talkeetna resident Bruce Hudson. Shaff had lived in Talkeetna—and loved the Fairview—for years, actually living in the Fairview for a number of those years. "When I was wiring that place one time—we were remodeling it—I'd go upstairs to do the wiring, and the switch would go off downstairs," Hudson says. "And nobody was touching it. So I'd go back upstairs, and it would go back off, and he was doing it, I know he was. That's just one ghost in the Fairview I know about. In the front corner room, that's where he lived. There's all kinds of ghost stories about him in there." Some of these stories can be found in Ron Wendt's *Haunted Alaska*, which was published by Epicenter Press in 2002.

But whoever it was Farina had seen, she says she "saw him a couple of times out of the corner of my eye in the back room when I was getting ready to close up and stuff—I'd be at the bar, by where the cash register is, and just turn, and he'd be like just walking through the back room. He was solid—I mean I thought he was a person in there. I'd go and check and there was nothing in there."

For Farina, who had as a child experienced a chilling ghost encounter in her grandfather's house, her experiences in the Fairview were by comparison "pretty mild."

But for Kim Hoiby, who also worked in the Fairview in the 1980s, several experiences she had on two different occasions while trying to overnight in the rooms above the bar were somewhat more intense. She was working three different jobs at the time, and living some distance from Talkeetna. "It happened to be a day that I had all three jobs scheduled," she says of the first experience. With a late night/early morning schedule, she decided to simply stay over at the Fairview and put herself in Room One, next to the bathroom.

"But in the middle of the night I started hearing something like someone walking down the hallway, outside the door, and I kind of fell back asleep," she says. "It was quiet. Then I started hearing bumps coming from Room Two—like footsteps and somebody walking around in there and moving furniture, hitting the walls, and it woke me up. And I was the only one up there that night, and I had never heard of any ghosts or anything and it kind of freaked me out. But I thought, well, maybe somebody had come in, and so I didn't think nothing more of it until I came downstairs [in the morning], and I checked the book to see if somebody had come in and I saw there was no one in the book. Then I mentioned it to whoever I was working with at the time and [whoever it was] said, 'Oh, that's just the ghost in Room Two,' and I laughed it off; I didn't think nothing of it. And I went yeah, okay, whatever."

Then eight years later, after not having given that night "another thought," Hoiby tried sleeping again in the Fairview, this time landing in Room Two itself. "It was the dead of winter," she says, "and I was working there three nights a week. And I was by myself—exhausted, you know, really tired.

"I went to sleep and I was layin' there, and I heard something kind of moving, and I just didn't feel like

I was alone. And I thought, *Aw, you're just creeping yourself out.* I fell asleep but later on I woke up to movement at the end of the bed; somebody was pushing down on the mattress at the end of the bed— it was pitch dark in there and I couldn't see it, but that's what it felt like—somebody was touching the end of the bed, there was pressure and it moved and I only heard the one thump, but it scared the shit out of me. I couldn't see it but I felt it—somebody tapping the end of the bed. And then the footsteps. And it scared me enough to where I checked myself out, locked the place up at three in the morning and drove home at three, four in the morning.

"I drove myself home that night because I was alone. But I lived out in the woods alone and I wasn't scared there. I just felt this presence."

Many years later, current Fairview employee Mark Ashworth was sharing a room with the bartender after a long night at the bar. At this point Ashworth had already had some interesting experiences in the Fairview, but his bartender friend, Jen, was a non-believer. Until the night she and Ashworth shared Room Three.

"Out of that room, people have told me what sounds like a bowling ball (from Room Four), going across the floor or something weird like that," Ashworth says.

"On that night—I wish I had heard it; I was totally passed out, and Jen had tried to wake me up—she was doing her crossword on the bed at three in the morning or something, and she said it scared her, and it sounded like a basketball kept hitting the wall. And the next day she's like, 'I was trying to wake you up; you were so passed out. . .I was so freaked out.'

"It was comforting to know that she finally believed in something that I knew was real."

Ashworth has had a number of experiences, including one cold winter night around Christmastime after the bar had closed when he was outside the side door smoking a cigarette and heard footsteps on the stairs beyond the closed door behind him. "I could hear the direction (of the steps) and they went around the corner, toward the bathrooms, and then I heard a door click, like a door shut," he says. "So I put out my cigarette, went inside, and nobody was there. I ran upstairs real fast to see if it could have been the three guests in the first room; I didn't see any activity or hear anything. So I can't say for sure, but the footsteps were very distinctive. And I never heard the steps go back up."

Another time Ashworth was sitting at the bar with a friend who also didn't believe that the Fairview is a haunted place. "It was wintertime years ago, and there were about three of us in the bar," he says. "I was just in the rest-room in here and that used to have a latch on it, the men's bathroom. And I heard it jiggling and I was washing my hands and I'm like, 'Wait,' and I opened the door real fast to be polite, and nobody was there. I walked over and nobody had moved. They'd have to be Spiderman to go that fast. So I sat there and told my friend how I was just in the bathroom and the door was jiggling and then we heard the side door slam and it was shut. We both looked over: not a soul." Ashworth says his friend started believing the stories after that.

Ashworth's Fairview experiences go back some nineteen years when he and another friend, Woody, were playing chess at a window table. "There was a black pawn missing, so we substituted it with a quarter," Ashworth says, noting that the pair had looked extensively for the missing pawn. "We looked behind the bar, we looked everywhere. . . and I had a quarter, so Woody substituted the missing pawn with a quarter, and I heard it roll to the right, and I looked at it, and the black pawn rolled out of nowhere from the direction of the wall and window toward the board and I looked at Woody and I said, 'That's not funny,' and he said, 'I didn't do that.'

Years later a long-time local resident heard Ashworth telling that story and said, "You know who used to sit at that table? Frank Moennikes; he used to sit there by himself playing chess."

"So about 15 years later I heard that part of the story," Ashworth says. Frank Moennikes, who had spent many years in Talkeetna beginning as far back as the 1930s, had owned the Fairview at one point for a period of 15 years.

Another story that was passed on to Ashworth came from Talkeetna radio talk show commentator and longtime member of the Talkeetna Bachelor Society, Gary Hermes, himself now passed. "Gary's story was that he was in the bar, and he said there was nobody in the rooms, and he checked the books because he heard water flowing—he was doing all the cleaning like I do in the morning," Ashworth says. "And so he goes upstairs to see who's up there, and that's when he noticed that there was water in the shower—I don't know if it was the iron tub or which—but then down the hallway there were wet footprints. And no person."

Figures at the bar. Footsteps on the stairs and in the hallway. Strange noises from the rooms. Doorknobs that jiggle by themselves and doors that close and slam on their own—sometimes with Ashworth or other employees present. And perhaps sometimes with nothing but the walls as witness.

The Restless Climber

The first summer of the new century found me in a transitional phase of my life. Having lost my mother unexpectedly four years earlier, I was finally starting to find my way out of the minefield that is grief, but the process had not been without its casualties: my marriage had tumbled into an awkward separation that became more permanent with each passing year, and my financial situation was such that I was working two jobs (three during the academic year) and spending several nights a week in a small unplumbed cabin in the backyard of my mother's still-mortgaged property. In addition to my cabin, which had been built elsewhere and I'd had moved to its then-current place, the property had the house my mother had lived in briefly before her death and a small cabin on the front yard corner, where my friends Chip and Michele Faurot had lived as tenants for many years prior to moving to their own property. Both the front cabin and the big house were fully rented. The summer was a busy one for me: I worked as news director for our local public radio station as well as news editor at our new and growing local newspaper, reporting on everything from village council meetings to tragic plane crashes in the Alaska Range.

It was in the first part of July (the "Saturday" of summer as I call it, with June being the Friday and August the Sunday) when I began experiencing strange sensations while I slept in my small loft bedroom. It began as the feeling of something like cat feet walking on my bed; I would be asleep but aware at the same time, the conscious part of me begging the unconscious part to wake up, to please, please wake up. And when I would, I would find nothing on the bed, or on the loft, or in the tiny cabin except myself—and my fiercely pounding heart.

This went on for nearly a week, in the early hours of morning it seemed, and I was beginning to become afraid of falling asleep at night. Then one night the feeling of something on my bed intensified—it was as if whatever it was, was trying to push itself into my whole body—I felt a pressing down on the length of me and the conscious part of me began screaming inside and crying out to my dead mother to help me, please help me. Then abruptly it stopped, and I woke up.

The following night I stayed awake as long as I could and slept for most of the night on the couch downstairs. But then before I knew it, it was morning, and there had been no cat feet—or anything else—on my bed. But as I woke further I realized there had been something. Part of my dream had been filled with images of letters from the alphabet— almost as if cut from the pages of a newspaper—and I remembered distinctly the letters "M" and "S." And there had been a voice: "I didn't mean to frighten you. I'm a climber; Michele knows me." Michele had recently opened her dream: Café Michele, located just before the start of Talkeetna's Main Street (and now under new ownership as the Kahiltna Bistro). I knew where to find her, but what would I say? In the light of day it all seemed so—odd. Embarrassing, even. And while in my mind I was actively entertaining the thought that I was being haunted, the safest place for that thought seemed to be just there—in my mind.

But another night, and another dream that didn't seem like a dream: It was just getting light and I sat up in my bed. I could feel I wasn't alone. I scooted across my mattress and looked over the edge of the loft. There was a man sitting at the bottom of my stairs, looking up at me and smiling.

I woke up. The light in my cabin was gray, just as it had been in my dream; frantically, I looked over the edge of the loft. Nothing. Nothing and no one.

It was Moose Dropping Festival weekend. I had a booth for my crafts (yet another job of mine): candles and beaded prisms, along with some incense and a few imports left over from a brief attempt at a store. The day went well and I stayed out late with much of the rest of the town and slept soundly and undisturbed that night. However, on Sunday evening, around nine o'clock when I was unloading the remains of my booth back into my cabin, out of the corner of my eye I saw something at the edge of the yard nearby. The shape of a shoulder, a glimpse of a white T-shirt. But there was no one there. "All right," I said out-loud. "I'll talk to Michele."

Several days later I had lunch with some coworkers at Café Michele, which was just down the street from the radio station. I was still debating inside whether or not to really talk to Michele. I had known Michele since I was nineteen years old when I met her and her then-partner, the writer Rick Leo, while we rode the train together from Anchorage to Talkeetna, and we shared a bond of having known our town in the quiet days before it became a tourist destination. Michele had been on hand during the days of my mother's sudden illness and, in fact, catered the reception after my mother's service; we had shared good times and bad over the many years we had known each other. And I knew Michele to be an open minded and spiritual person. But in the light of day this seemed so over the top, and at the end of lunch I still wasn't sure. Then I saw her, behind her front counter, and she was wearing a white T-shirt, and the T-shirt was like a neon sign telling me I had to talk to her.

I can't remember exactly how I said it, but I didn't have to say much. She flinched as if someone had punched her in the stomach, put a hand to her mouth and said without a moment's hesitation: "Oh my God, it's Mugs." And then I knew, that whoever Mugs was he had returned to the property where Michele had once lived looking for her—and found me instead.

I learned this: Terrance "Mugs" Stump was a McKinley guide based out of Talkeetna in the early 1990s—during a time I lived in Anchorage—was a somewhat notorious womanizer and was close friends with Michele, who was devastated after he died suddenly when a serac collapsed beneath him while he was descending McKinley at the end of a successful guided climb in 1992. He was 42 years old.

"I've felt him lately," Michele had said that day.

She added that Mugs was a "restless spirit" and that she'd felt his presence before.

After talking to Michele, I finally shared the story with other friends; one told me there was a picture of Mugs on the wall in the lounge of the recently built Talkeetna Alaskan Lodge. I didn't waste much time going up to the lodge to see it. As I entered the lounge I saw large framed photos on the far wall. But I didn't need to read the nameplates to know which one was him. From across the room I recognized him: the man at the bottom of my stairs.

I saw Mugs in a dream one time after that. He was—strangely—dressed in a purple wizard robe, much like one in my son's old costume box. I asked him if there was anything I could do for him—if he wanted me to write about him. He said he liked attention, so I could do that if I wanted, but no—he didn't need me to do anything. And I never saw him again—this man I never knew. But I never forgot him, or those strange weeks in July, and now and again I wander over to the Talkeetna Cemetery where, not far from the Climbers' Memorial, a small slab of granite reads:

Terry Manbeck Stump
Beloved "Mugs"

August 1949-May 1992
His grave—
the South Buttress
His spirit free—
Ever within our hearts.

Down on the Farm

The Lichtenwalner farm lies off the Talkeetna Spur Road along the railroad tracks slightly south of town. The property was originally owned by a trapper named Erling Floe, who later sold it to a farmer named Milt Lichtenwalner. Lichtenwalner built a new structure on the property separate from Floe's original cabin and operated a working farm there until dying suddenly of a heart attack in 1979.

In the early 1970s, my younger sister and I used to leave our cabin in the woods for trips to the home of Talkeetna artist Jim Gleason and his wife, Bev, who resided in Floe's old cabin, so we could take drawing lessons from Jim. The cabin eventually was sold, along with a portion of the farm's acreage, to Ken and Mary Farina who lived in it until they built a larger home on the property for their growing family.

It was while Ken and Mary still lived in the little cabin that Sandy Shoulders befriended them in the mid 1980s when she was new to town and working with Mary at the Fairview, a "rite of passage," Mary says, for newcomers. Shoulders has since gone on to found Talkeetna's Music Academy, part of the Denali Arts Council, and its Red Shoes Orchestra.

But back in the '80s, at one point the Farinas were going out of town and asked Shoulders to house-sit. "I don't know if it was for a week or whatever it was," Shoulders says. "So I did, and of course I had no idea what the house was about; I didn't know it was by the railroad tracks. So that was a whole bunch of fright right there, hearing the first freight train come through in the middle of the night."

But there was something much more frightening to come. The bedroom of the cabin was upstairs in the loft, and one night while sleeping there Shoulders woke to a surprising sight. "I woke up, and I sat up in bed, and there was the figure of a man, standing at the foot of the bed. I just kind of sat up and there he was.

"And it was unmistakable, absolutely unmistakable. And he was moving just enough that I could tell that it was actually somebody—he wasn't stone-still.

"He didn't say anything, but he was there, and then he was gone. And it was quite frightening, and so I remember sitting up in the bed awhile, not knowing exactly what to do and I think I probably got up and went downstairs and turned on some lights or something. But it was unmistakably a man standing at the foot of the bed." It was too dark for Shoulders to distinguish any features. "I wouldn't be able to recognize a picture or anything," she says. "It seems like he was maybe in a bulky coat—a regular Talkeetna kind of guy. And he wasn't giant; he was just average size." But, she says, "He was *somebody*. And maybe he just wanted to know who was sleeping in his bed. I don't know.

"I think between that and the trains I said I'd never stay again. That was a little too much for me."

Longtime Talkeetna resident Johnny Baker, who purchased from Lichtenwalner's heirs the part of the farm not owned by the Farinas, knew Erling Floe and said he was a tall man of Finnish descent; Shoulders says the figure she saw wasn't that tall, so perhaps it was the shorter Lichtenwalner returning to his beloved property to check on things.

And Baker recalls, with a laugh, how Lichtenwalner *did* return to the farm after his death—in a round about sort of way:

"I ran into Bob Husted [who used to stay at the farm] one time, and he said, 'Did I ever tell you about finding Milt hangin' on a fence?' And you know, it doesn't make sense in English, it doesn't make a good sentence. So I said, 'How could you possibly find

Milt hanging on a fence?"

"There were fences all around that property. Well anyway, he says, 'I was walkin' back through one of the fields to the woods, along one of these fences, and I found this bag, hanging on the fence.' And he says, 'As soon as I saw it I knew what it was. It was Milt's ashes.'

"They threw the ashes out of the airplane," Baker says. "They wanted them to go onto the farm, but they thought the bag was going to open up. . .What are the *odds* of something like that?"

But Baker did have two less explainable experiences on the farm in the cabin Lichtenwalner built.

"When I was redoin' that cabin, I was right down to just bare walls and everything, tearing out the walls," he says. "And I was under the sink doing something. And I heard something slide across the wall and fall on the floor. And I said, you know, that sounds like a broom or a shovel falling, 'cause I had everything in there. But I was busy under the sink doing something, and all of a sudden, I heard something slip and fall and hit the floor again. I said, 'Now this can't happen twice in a row.' So I went in and sat on a sawhorse, and I said, 'Hey, if there's something goin' on here or around here, all right, I'm payin' attention now, tell me what you want.' But nothing ever fell that I could ever find that hit the floor. And nobody ever answered me."

Several years later, Baker was napping in the renovated farmhouse. "I was sleeping on the couch, and I felt something touch my leg," he says. "It was like about maybe three fingers. And I felt the touch, then it moved up and touched me again, and I'm thinking: *This is a bit strange. If it does that one more time, I'm going to turn over.* I had my back to it; I was going to turn over and see. . .but it never did it again."

And there's another story connected to the Lichtenwalner farm, this one again at the small original cabin, back in the days when Jim and Bev Gleason still resided there. That story, written by Jonathan, is as follows:

Throughout my life I've been searching out spooky stories of the Alaskan bush. One of the themes that keeps coming up is voices out of nowhere. Sure, some of these phantom voice encounters are due to mis-identification—animal or bird sounds. Others can be attributed to cabin fever, but there remains those that can't be explained.

The far north is a land that has witnessed hardship, suffering, violence and tragedy for thousands of years. There is no question in my mind that there are restless souls wandering the muskeg and black spruce. Think of all the missing planes, lost hunters, Athabascan warriors lost in battle or to grizzly bears. The northern bush has a million horrible ways to kill you. Yes, there are lost ghosts wandering through the wilderness.

I was house-sitting, with my then girlfriend Julie Gleason, her parents' place on the old Lichtenwalner farm.

It was a cold, drizzly, late spring night. Julie and I were quietly reading when we suddenly heard voices coming up the trail. We exchanged puzzled looks— who in the world could be visiting at this time of night in this weather? We clearly heard them talking, approaching the cabin, right up to the door. I opened the door, ready to welcome whoever it was out on such a night, but no one was there. I stepped out and called, "Hello! We're home!" I walked around the cabin: nothing. Then I walked down the trail, out to the railroad tracks: nothing. My "spidey senses" began sending the alarm as a chill went through me. I went back to the cabin and grabbed my rifle. "What's up? Where are they?" Julie asked.

"I don't know. Something's weird," I replied. I told her I was going to look around a little bit and to stay alert. I also told her not to let anyone in because whoever it was, was out hiding around the cabin. That could not be good.

I spent the next thirty minutes stealthily patrolling the perimeter. I looked everywhere; there not only was nobody out there, but there were no tracks in the spring mud. I went back to the cabin, locked the door, and settled in for a restless night with my rifle within easy reach. Thirty-five years later, I still can't figure it out.

The Man
at the Late Night Bar

"Ghosts are a fact, but not all ghosts are discarnate spirits of the departed," writes paranormal writer and scholar Paul Roland in his book, *The Complete Book of Ghosts: A Fascinating Exploration of the Spirit World, from Apparitions to Haunted Places.* The book, as Roland states, "accepts apparitions as a natural phenomenon" and takes the concept of ghosts a little further, stating that at times what we believe is a ghost is the spirit of someone still living, temporarily set loose from the physical body during states of intense relaxation or severe crisis. Taking that into consideration, maybe at times that there-then-gone glimpse of a figure or flash of a face might not originate from somewhere beyond the grave; however, when what we see matches up with a who-that-used-to-be-but-is-no-more, our thoughts turn ghostly. Such was the case when a local river guide and his friends made a late-night stop at the Tee Pee Lounge, part of the Talkeetna Motel, a local haven just around the bend and off the beaten track from a busy summertime Main Street.

"I've never seen a ghost before or anything," says Bill Barstow, who at the time of the forthcoming event was working as a river guide. Out on the town, Barstow and his friends ended up at the Tee Pee. "We went to the right side [of the room] and I looked over at the corner of the bar—on the corner diagonally across from us—and I saw this guy—a smallish guy with long kind of curly hair, and he was drinking whiskey. In one of those short glasses. He was looking at me and I said to my friend, 'Ross, see that guy over there? Drinking a whiskey?' And Ross was like, 'Uh, no.' And I'm like, 'Yeah—over there. He's toasting us right now.' But Ross didn't see anyone." When Barstow looked away, then looked back, the man was gone.

"I don't know why I would put that in my head if I didn't see it—why I would imagine it," he says. "It was kind of weird. There was this guy, lifting his whiskey glass and toasting. I don't know why I would have suddenly decided someone was at the corner of the bar if there wasn't."

When Barstow told me this story, long before I'd decided to write this book, I couldn't help but think that his description of the mysteriously disappearing man at the bar sounded uncannily like a former resident who used to play drums in rock and roll bands with my brothers and who died tragically a number of years ago in a freak drowning accident while he was working, like Barstow, as a river guide on the local rivers. In the years prior to his death he lived near the Tee Pee and was a frequent late-night visitor.

And when I asked my brother Jonathan what sort of drink this fellow was likely to have, he said: "Oh—that's easy. Whiskey and water. And always in a short glass."

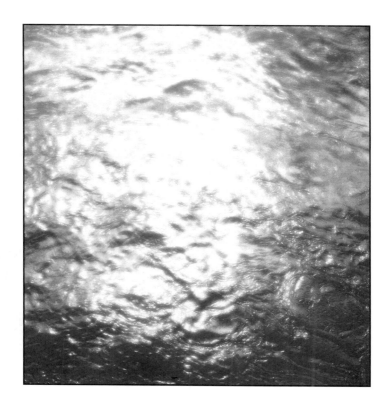

Not Alone at Nagley's

When I was a teenager, Nagley's Trading Post was called the B&K and was owned by a woman named Adele Shaff. Its log walls were part of a store once located in the long faded settlement of Susitna Station; original owner Horace Nagley moved the business to Talkeetna in the early 1920s and reestablished it in the still young but growing town. In the 1940s, under new ownership, the store became the B&K, but it has since been restored to its original name by the current owner, who also added the West Rib Pub & Grill onto the building where Tim Rose was working late one night when something a little out of the ordinary occurred.

"I guess I'd start by saying that at night by myself, I never felt *alone* at Nagley's—especially not in the downstairs," Rose says, adding that the store's basement is known as the "Dead Man Room" in a nod to local lore which suggests that bodies were stored there in the winter while waiting burial. "I always felt when you opened the door to go to Nagley's at night by yourself, it was kind of creepy. But I felt that way before this night. . .just kind of uneasy."

The night Rose remembers was a fall night, late August or early September, a time when local residents get the first glimpse of the deep dark nights ahead. Rose says it was sometime after midnight and he and two other employees were in the process of having a beer and closing up. "There was a sound—I think initially maybe a train went by—but then it was real loud for awhile and at the end of the sound we heard a crash—it was in the liquor store and I went like, what the hell is that?" Rose says. He and one of the other employees went into the liquor store where "a bunch a things had fallen from baskets that were hanging above the counter" and items that had been in baskets on the counter had flipped off the counter and onto the floor. "There was a four-pack of little wine bottles that had come from on top of the counter and landed five feet from the counter upside down, but all still together. How did that happen, you know?

"We put it all back and then went back into the pub, but it freaked us both out pretty good."

Rose recalls another employee who said she was "talking to the ghosts" when he heard her talking in the "Dead Man Room" where items for the store and the pub were stored. "One time she was talking and I'd said, 'Who are you talking to?'" Rose says. "And she'd said, 'Oh, the spirits. I just want to let them know I'm down here and I'm okay and things are going good.'

"I could relate because I always had this feeling and had that experience," Rose says. "So I wasn't alone. It was unsettling in the store—especially in the basement."

Michael London, who was with Rose the night strange things happened in the liquor store (and who doesn't remember the noise, but does remember witnessing some shot glasses and other items come off a shelf above the cash register), says he always thought Nagley's might be haunted by the ghost of a cat. "Things were always getting knocked over as if a cat was running by," he says. And while Nagley's is the home of Talkeetna's honorary and somewhat famous "mayor" Stubbs the Cat, London says before Stubbs there was Squeek, and there was also the Nagley's fire of 1997 when a morning blaze broke out in the historic landmark. "When Nagley's was burning, folks were standing out front when someone asked if anyone had seen Squeek," London says. "Nobody had, when suddenly the cat came running out the front door to everyone's relief." But as the story goes, at that moment a fire engine "came roaring around the corner, the cat did a 180 and ran back into the burning building. Squeek was never seen again."

The Radiant
Woman in White

"Okay, I'll tell you what I saw," says longtime Talkeetna resident Chris Mannix, who over the years has served on the Talkeetna Community Council, the local trails committee and as a founding member of the Denali Nordic Ski Club. One night when his wife, Barbara, was out of town, Mannix was celebrating a friend's 60th birthday party at the Alaska Mountaineering School building, housed in what was previously the town's Baptist church. The building is located near the Talkeetna Cemetery, across the railroad tracks from the main townsite. The school, founded and led by Caitlin Palmer and Colby Coombs, modified the old building to accommodate the school's instructional courses and guided climb operation. But many Talkeetna residents remember the building as a place of church services, weddings, and funerals.

"Anyway," Mannix says of the night in question, "there was a big birthday party going on—singing and dancing and all that kind of stuff. And at the end of the evening I didn't feel like driving home, and at that

time the building was set up with two bedrooms upstairs, and so Colby said, 'You can stay here.'

"I was the only one in the building. Everyone had
gone home and the lights were shut off and I crawled
into bed, went to sleep and sometime in the middle of
the night I woke from a dead sleep—I guess I kind of
sensed that someone had come into the room, and I
sat up in bed and I looked over and in the door there
was this woman dressed in white, and she was. . .radi-
ant, dressed in a long white dress; she was just there
and I think I turned to her and said, 'Who are you?'

"I can't remember now if I even got a response—
but when I sat up, there was eye contact—and then
she turned and left. I heard her go down the stairs. . .
so I turned on the lights and I went down and I looked
in every room in the building and there was no one
there and it was totally bizarre, you know—and so in
the middle of the night I got up and left.

"The next morning I asked Caitlin if anyone was
around. Her mom had been staying in the house
next door, but she hadn't been out and about. So it
was just this random, unexplainable thing. It was
really bizarre. This was not a dream by any stretch
of the imagination. . .there she was, and then there
she wasn't."

The Harry Robb Cabin

"In all the old places in town, it seemed there was something out of the ordinary, and I'd just gotten kind of hardened to it, I guess," says Marty Terstegge, who over his years in Talkeetna, both as a carpenter and as part of the Talkeetna Historical Society, found himself often being part of the remodellings and renovations of some of Talkeetna's oldest buildings. "If it was anything more than 'Oh, I think I heard a voice' or something like that, I'd say, 'Go away, leave me alone, I'm working.' And then I'd go back to work."

But when the Talkeetna Historical Society bought for a dollar the old cabin last owned by Talkeetna "old timer" Harry Robb, the "time capsule" the cabin had become since Robb's death contained more than just Robb's former possessions. "I did see one [a ghost] in there walking across the room and I assumed it was Harry," Terstegge says, remembering the moment when he and Talkeetna Historical Society board member Myron Stevens were the first ones in the cabin since it was closed up after Robb's death in 1976.

"It had been locked up for 25 years and his pants—his black pair of pants—were laying there on the bed." It was as if Robb had simply walked out the door. "He was sick, and the people who found him took him to Anchorage and he didn't come back," Terstegge says.

Robb, a former riverboat pilot, had bought the two-story log cabin sometime in the 1930s from a man named Dave Lawrence who built the cabin in 1924. Robb spent the rest of his life there.

And though Terstegge only saw that initial glimpse of a figure walking across the room, he couldn't shake a strange feeling as he prepared the cabin to become part of the historical society's collection. "There was a funny feeling to that project the whole time," he says, adding that in the Robb building, as well as the other old Talkeetna buildings Terstegge worked on, he's "never felt anything evil; I never got an evil feeling, just a surprise—kind of a 'Oh, huh'—like I was surprised and they were surprised." But with the Robb cabin, he says, "That whole project stuck in my mind."

Late Nights, Strange Sights, and Thoughts of Evil Alice

If you go down the length of Talkeetna's Main Street and follow it around the curve past the National Park Service's Talkeetna Ranger Station, you'll find the Talkeetna Motel and its adjacent Tee Pee Lounge quietly embedded in the life and lore of the town. Originally built by a woman named Alice Powell who somewhere along the line was nicknamed "Evil Alice" (perhaps it has to do with a 1969 court case in which she tried to collect damages for injuries she suffered as a passenger on a snowmachine-ride-gone-wrong), the unique complex eventually became the property of Al Sousa and his longtime companion, Pam Allman, who own and operate the place to this day. And though Allman's been there now for over 20 years, and Powell had long left Talkeetna and her beloved Tee Pee behind before passing away in 1992, Allman says she's sometimes not at all certain Alice is truly gone.

"I feel like I'm possessed sometimes because I will work hours and hours and hours and I don't seem to really get tired, maybe mentally fatigued, but body-wise I just keep going," Allman says. "My personality is to do things to my very best anyway, and I'm also obsessive-compulsive; in my older age I see myself getting more and more so—everything's got to be just a certain way. So that's a lot of my own nature, but at the same time I definitely have a heart for this old building and I'm not sure why, and that part of it I think was Alice's dream, too, that she had when she built it, and I think some of that's passed on to me somehow through her."

But one late night, while working alone in the kitchen, Allman's thoughts of Alice took a more substantive form. "To see something when you're not expecting it, and you're not looking for something and it makes you turn, it makes you feel like. . .you know," she says. "I get cold bumps when I think about it.

"It was around '98, '99; we were down to short staff and I did a lot of prep for the work staff in the kitchen. Sometimes if I was bartending—if I was a fill-in late at night—I would leave the bar after I was done and go into the restaurant and finish up whatever needed to be chopped up or prepped up for the next day. Sometimes it was just setting up—napkins and whatever, but I happened to be at the cook's counter chopping—I think I was doing onions or something—

and I was sitting there busy chopping and thinking about what was going to happen the next day, trying to hash it over in my head so it was *right* in there the next morning when I got up.

"It was probably about 2:30 or so, maybe 3 o'clock in the morning, and there are no windows in the A-frame kitchen anywhere so there's no external way for any light to come in. I was in a fluorescent-lit room, and the kitchen was bright, but over to the right of me there's a walkway that goes around to the back ice room all the way to the kitchen and then into the wait station and dining room area. Off of that just a little catiwhompus up ahead and to my right was the walk-in cooler, I call it: the pantry that you step down into and then you go into the walk-in cooler. We were in the process of remodeling and Al had the ceiling open a little bit to get to the wiring because we'd done a new island. So the florescent light off the very right that sat angled where the different roof [of the building] was, was totally down; we'd pulled the bulbs out of it. So it was a little dimmer on that side of the room.

"So I was chopping and just thinking about things and all of a sudden I kind of got a chilled feeling and as that happened this light, kind of elongated, let's say a couple of feet high, just passed and caught my attention. . .I looked and it was just very quietly and fairly fast moving out into the dining room area, just this spirit—it was kind of dim yellow but long, like I say, two feet high, and it wasn't just solid, it was abstract along the edges—it was kind of luminous in the center and kind of cloudy on the outside; that's the best I can describe it. It just passed through from the back ice room off on my right side into the dining room and disappeared. I just kind of stood there like, oh my God, you know."

Though her mother had recently passed and Allman considers the possibility that the form she saw might have been her mother's spirit, she says she always feels that "Alice is here—I just really do; every once in awhile I'll just get a feeling here, you know" though she's never seen the luminous apparition since. "I have no idea what that light might have been," she says, "but it definitely happened. I get cold chills right now thinking about it."

Another night yielded a different type of frightening experience. "The whole bar was closed down, it was late; we would stay open until 5 a.m., and it was dark so it would have been maybe late September, no snow yet outside," she says. "The top part of the A-frame that houses the lounge has an open area toward the back, about three-quarters away from the south end of the building back here to just one big room and it has big wooden shelves that were actually built into the structure, and we had all kinds of stuff up there, old antiques or whatever.

"But anyway that night, everything was secure up there, nothing was going to come off the shelf. I was done with the bar, I was sitting down, all the lights were turned off out front and everything, and I was doing up my paperwork at the end of the bar, and that was during a time where there really wasn't anybody living too much down this end of the world; there wasn't anybody close by. So when it got dark and late I was pretty much the only one on this end of town. But I got used to it, after all the years of working here, and I was good with being by myself down here.

"So I started the paperwork; I was posting things, and all of a sudden up above me, kind of like in the middle of the bar area, I heard three steps, and they were heavy steps, like one, two, three—it wasn't just like the floor creaking; it was like, three heavy steps. And it immediately made me think somebody had come in—there were stairs on the back of the lounge building and there was a door up there—but besides being locked it had a board nailed across it—but my first thought was that somebody had come in that door. . .

"So I got off of my chair, real quickly. It was dark and I wasn't going to go up there by myself. So I was thinking, okay, I'm sitting at this end of the bar, the sound I just heard is right above me; if the person came in the back door and they were going to come down the spiral stairs, I'm going to be out the back door and in my car and gone home. I can lock the back door and get myself out of the building. It scared me so bad that I wasn't even thinking about the safety of the building much at that point, so I opened up the back door real quickly and I looked and that door [to the upstairs area] was totally in place. There was no room for it to open. I came back in and I just stood by the back doorway and watched for a couple of seconds and I listened, and there wasn't anything else. There were no more steps, there was no more anything. At that point I left my paperwork and everything, got into my car and went home.

"The next day I went up and checked. Nothing was on the floor, nothing had been tipped over. And I never heard any sounds up there since then, either. But no telling—and they were definitely footsteps; I'm a very practical person. Whoever it might have been, was just roaming around."

Toughluck

I've tried to avoid, putting into this book, stories that have no witness—no one to step forward and say, "This is what I saw/heard/experienced." But I can't help but mention the story of Toughluck, even though I haven't been able to substantiate the legend.

This much I know is true: George Toughluck, who lived in a cabin with his family across the railroad tracks from where the old depot once sat, was hit by a train and killed. He was buried—and his grave still remains—on a stretch of land that lies between the railroad tracks and the east side of town, the Dena'ina Indian "spirit house" which had sat on top of the burial site long since fallen to vandalism and the elements. The home that once stood nearby, and where his surviving wife and children had continued to live, either burned down sometime after his death or eventually succumbed to disrepair and the elements.

Now to the legend: Toughluck was beheaded in the accident, and his headless ghost can be seen wandering the train tracks near where he died and where his old home stood.

Pat Pratt, the daughter of legendary Talkeetna "old timer" Jim Beaver, played, as a kid in the 1950s, with Toughluck's children. "I was like four or five and I remember going over there," Pratt says. "And then it would kind of be getting twilight, we'd be out playing, and I'd have to go past that little grave house of his and it had the little window in it and things sitting inside. . .Oh, God, I used to just run so fast, I just knew something was going to get me. Every time I walk over there now I just recall, you know, sixty years ago when I was a kid fantasizing about something coming out of that little grave."

Toughluck's grave can still be found, if one knows where to look, amongst the bushes and trees of a stretch of land that keeps growing and changing and moving forward without him.

Or maybe not.

Four books were indispensable during the writing of this one: *The Heritage of Talkeetna* by Roberta Sheldon (Talkeetna Editions, 1995); *A River Between Us* by Ken Marsh (Trapper Creek Museum Sluice Box Productions, 2002); *Talkeetna Cronies* by Nola Campbell (Color Art Printing Co., 1974); and *Knik, Matanuska, Susitna: A Visual History of the Valleys* by Vickie Cole, Pat O'Hara, Pandora Willingham, Ron Wendt, and Mary Simpson (Bentwood Press, 1985).

Other sources are *Shem Pete's Alaska* by James Kari and James A. Fall (University of Alaska Press, 1987); *The Complete Book of Ghosts: A Fascinating Exploration of the Spirit World, from Apparitions to Haunted Places* by Paul Roland (Chartwell Books, 2007); and *Minus 148°* by Art Davidson (Mountaineers Books, 1999).

Alaska Range climbing statistics were retrieved from the National Park Service website at http://www. nps.gov/dena/planyourvisit/current-statistics.htm; details of the death of Mugs Stump were garnered from the 1992 Mountaineering Summary on the same site.